FRIENDS
by Kathryn Cave and Nick Maland

Text copyright © Kathryn Cave 2004
Illustrations copyright © Nick Maland 2004

The right of Kathryn Cave to be identified as
the author and Nick Maland as the illustrator of
this work has been asserted by them in accordance
with the Copyright, Designs and Patents Act 1988.

First published by Hodder Children's Books 2004.
This edition published by Friendly Dragon 2015.

www.friendly-dragon.com

A catalogue record for this book is available
from the British Library.

ISBN 978-0-99310-780-1

Printed in China

The illustrations in this book
were made with watercolour
on photocopied drawings

10 9 8 7 6 5 4 3 2 1

*For my dear friends, past, present and future.* **K.C.**

*For my friends, Mark and Johnny.* **N.M.**

# Friends

Written by **Kathryn Cave**

Illustrated by **Nick Maland**

FRIENDLY DRAGON
BOOKS

Once I was lost
in the wood,
in the wood,

and you
found me.

Once I fell down.
I hurt my knee.
You put your arms round me.

Once I was shy,
I didn't know where to go,
until you saw me.

Once I was slow,
I couldn't catch up.
You waited for me.

Once I was afraid
of the dark, of the dark,
and the creatures that
hide there.

You didn't laugh
and it wasn't so bad,
with you at my side there.

Once I got cross.
I really yelled.
You got cross, too.

When I stopped being cross,
I felt sad and alone.
I thought I'd lost you.

# But I hadn't.

*'Want to be friends?'*

'OK.'

If you are lost
in the wood, in the wood,
I will find you.

If you're afraid
of the cold and the dark,
I'll sit beside you.

I'll wait for you,
I'll share with you,
I'll comfort you,
I'll care for you
the way you cared for me.

That's what friends do.